WRITTEN AND CREATED BY
RUSSELL NOHELTY

PENCILS AND COVERS BY
JUAN FRIGERI

COLORS BY
THOMAS BACON

INKS BY
FERNANDO MELEK

LETTERS BY
BERNIE LEE

DEDICATED TO SUSAN, WHO FIGHTS HARDER FOR WHAT SHE BELIEVES IN THAN ANY PERSON I KNOW.

VERY SPECIAL THANKS TO

JAMES NOHELTY   SEAN SEXTON   PETE TORRES

SPECIAL THANKS

ANDREW RACHO, YOU ARE A ROCK STAR!
PAUL FERREIRA, CAAAAAAAAAAAAAAKE!
JAMES NOHELTY, DUDES FOR DADS ROCK. GET ONE!
GREY WEARS, PUPPETS FOR LIFE!
MIKA KOYKKA, GREETINGS FROM HELL!
CRIS TIEFENWORTH, THANK YOU FOR THE SUPPORT!
ZACH KLUE, THANK YOU SO MUCH!
VIKTOR PASTOR, YOU ARE AWESOME!
IN MEMORY OF LUKE. THAT GUY HAD IT ALL.
KATRINA LOVES RICHARD RIVERA! THANKS!
SHELLEY SMITH, LONG LIVE CREATIVITY!
KAISA LINDGREN, MAY THE ZOMBIES BE ON YOUR SIDE!
SPECIAL THANKS TO BART VERSTREKEN.
SPECIAL THANKS TO DAVE BAXTER!
THANK YOU BOBBY FOR SUPPORTING THE KICKSTARTER
        FOR KATRINA HATES THE DEAD!
THANK YOU LIAM. P.S KHT WUZ HERE 2015.
PAUL JARMAN, YOU ARE A ROCK STAR! THANK YOU!
THANKS BRANDON FOR YOUR UNDYING SUPPORT!
ANDREW ROBINSON! THANKS FOR THE SUPPORT! KATRINA'S
        CHOSEN YOU FOR HER ZOMBIE-APOCALYPSE TEAM.
NICK WILLIAMS, THANKS FOR YOUR SUPPORT!
THANKS NIRAJ!
THANKS BRIAN DE CONINCK! THE DE CONINCK FAMILY
        HATES THE DEAD, JUST AS MUCH AS KATRINA.
TO BIG G, ENJOY!
TO THE BRILLIANT AND SUPREMELY TALENTED
        ALLISON BARROWS, WITHOUT WHOM LIFE WOULD
        NOT BE WORTH LIVING.
TODD GOOD, THANK YOU SO MUCH FOR PLEDGING!
BRANDON BOOTH, YOU COULDN'T BE COOLER IF YOU
        STOOD IN A FREEZER FOR A MONTH. YOU'D BE
        DEAD THOUGH...THEN KATRINA WOULD HATE YOU.
TOMMY, YOU'RE THE GREATEST, MOST WONDERFUL
        PERSON IN THE WHOLE WORLD, THANK YOU!
GRADY SMITH, YOU ARE THE BEST! THANK YOU!
BRUCE HENNIGAN, THANK YOU SO MUCH!!!!
CHRISTIAN OH, THANKS BUDDY. YOU'RE AWESOME!
MOM, I CAN'T TELL YOU WHAT YOUR SUPPORT MEANS.
        THANK YOU!

TWO YEARS AGO...
...THE WORLD WENT THROUGH THE END OF TIMES.
THE APOCALYPSE. THE RAPTURE.
CHARLES!
OR WHATEVER YOU RELIGIOUS TYPES CALL IT.
THE GOOD BOYS AND GIRLS WERE BEAMED UP TO SOME GIANT ORGY IN THE SKY.
KAREN!
ANNIE!
LINDA!
TED!
LEAVING US REGULAR JOES AND JOETTES TO FEND FOR OURSELVES AND ASK ONE QUESTION.
WHY NOT ME?

THE DEAD ROSE FROM THEIR GRAVES.
A RIFT OPENED IN THE DESERT. ALL MANNER OF HELLSPAWN POURED OUT INTO THE WORLD.
AHHH!
BOY WERE THEY GLAD TO ESCAPE THE HEAT OF DAMNATION.
IT WAS BEDLAM, HELL ON EARTH.
GOD, PLEASE HELP ME!
THERE WAS NOTHING WE COULD DO TO STOP THEM.
UNTIL ONE DAY THEY GOT BORED AND OPTED FOR A QUIET LIFE IN THE SUBURBS.

MONSTERS SQUATTED IN THE HOMES OF THE PEOPLE THEY ONCE MERCILESSLY MURDERED.
THEY ARE NEITHER PLEASANT NOR POLITE NEIGHBORS.
DHUHAAAAHAHHH!
SHUT UP!
WHAT I GET YOU?
JUST A SMALL MEAL FOR MY SON.
IF THAT WASN'T ENOUGH THEY TOOK ALL THE GOOD GODDAMN JOBS.
SMALL MEAL!
LEAVING US TO STARVE AND DIE. THE LUCKY ONES AT LEAST.
THE REST OF US GOT ALONG ANY WAY WE COULD. EVEN AFTER WE'D LOST EVERYTHING.

INSIDE KATRINA'S APARTMENT. PRESENT.
GO AWAY!
SLAM SLAM
RING RING
HOWL
YEAH. YOU DON'T LIKE THAT DO YOU?!
WHAT RONALD?
DAMN KATRINA, IT'S LOUD OVER THERE. SOMEBODY HITTIN' THAT?
YOU THINK I'D ANSWER A CALL FROM MY BOSS IF I WAS HAVING SEX?
I'D LIKE TO THINK SO. LISTEN BRO, YOU GOTTA COME IN.
IT'S MY DAY OFF.
DON'T KNOW WHAT TO TELL YOU. KIM AND ALEX BOTH CAUGHT THE PLAGUE. CAN'T HAVE THEM WORKING WITH FOOD SINCE THEY'RE LIKE, DEAD.
I HATE YOU.
EASY PIZZA

I KICKED YOU OUT TWO WEEKS AGO, BARRY. NOW PISS OFF.
ENOUGH!
CLICK
I WANT MY TV. I JUST FOUND DONALD IN MATHMAGIC LAND AND I WANNA WATCH THAT SHIT.

I HAVEN'T SEEN A DIME FROM YOU IN SIX MONTHS. CONSIDER THE TV MY PAYMENT.
I'LL JUST KEEP COMING BACK. WE BOTH KNOW HOW MUCH YOU LOVE SEEING ME.
SIGH. TAKE THE TV AND YOU'RE OUT OF MY LIFE FOREVER. AGREED?
SCOUT'S HONOR. NOW LET ME IN. I'M FREEZING MY NERPS OFF.
FINE. GRAB IT AND GET OUT. I'M LATE ALREADY.
HEY. CAN I WALK WITH YOU? IT'S NOT SAFE OUT THERE AT NIGHT.
YOU'VE GOTTA BE KIDDING ME.

WAIT UP. THIS THING IS HEAVY.
SOUND JUST LIKE MY SISTER.
SHE STILL SACRIFICING GOATS TO THE DARK LORD?
YEAH, BUT IT'LL PASS. CONNIE'S JUST PISSED OUR DOUCHE BAG DAD GOT BLUE LIGHTED AND NOT HER.
YOU WANT TO WALK WITH ME. NOT THE OTHER WAY AROUND. SO KEEP UP OR GET LOST.
SHE NEEDS TO GET OVER IT.
YOU'RE ALL HEART.
I LET YOU MOVE IN, DIDN'T I?
BECAUSE YOU PITIED ME. COULD'VE JUST GIVEN ME A HANDIE AND CALLED IT A DAY.
AHHH!
SHUNK!
COME ON! UNCOOL!
THAT LOOKS PAINFUL.
GET IT OUT!
HOLD STILL. THIS IS GONNA STING.
YAAAAH!

HOW DOES IT LOOK?
GROAN
TERRIBLE.
WHAT WAS THAT?
JUST THE WIND.
DOESN'T SOUND LIKE THE WIND.
GROAN
GROAN
UGH.
GROAN.
DOESN'T LOOK LIKE THE WIND EITHER.
JUST SOME ZOMBOIDS. SCRAM, VAMOOSE. WE DON'T WANT NONE A WHATCH'RE SELLIN.
OH GOD. WE'RE GONNA DIE!
HA. YOU'RE FUNNY. NOT LIKE IT'S A DEMON.

WHAT ARE YOU DOING?
FIGHTING.

BUT THEY'LL RIP YOU APART.

PLEASE. THEY ARE THE DUMBEST, SLOWEST MONSTERS ON THE PLANET.

YOUR FUNERAL. JUST REMEMBER TO STAB THEM THROUGH THE BRAI-

SHUNK

THE BRAIN. I KNOW, BARRY. BARRY? OH THAT'S IT. LET'S GO!

SEE. TOLD YOU THEY WERE PUSSIES, BARRY. OH RIGHT, YOU'RE DEAD.
BRAVO.
CLAP CLAP
THOSE REALLY WERE THE MOST ANNOYING MOUTH BREATHERS I'VE EVER HAD THE DISPLEASURE TO SUPERVISE. THANK YOU FOR SENDING THEM BACK TO HELL.
CLAP CLAP CLAP CLAP
WHAT ARE YOU DOING HERE, THOMAS?
I WANT YOU BACK.
YOU NEVER HAD ME TO BEGIN WITH. NEWSFLASH, IF YOU'VE GOTTA SHAPESHIFT AND TRICK A CHICK INTO BANGING YOU IT'S JUST NOT MEANT TO BE.
THAT'S NEVER STOPPED ME BEFORE. BESIDES, WE WERE ELECTRIC TOGETHER.
IT WAS ONE NIGHT. TAKE ANOTHER STEP AND I'LL STAB YOU THROUGH THE THROAT.
MY DEAR. I'M NOT A ZOMBIE OR EVEN A VAMPIRE.
MORTAL WEAPONS WON'T KILL ME.

CAN'T FOOL ME, THOMAS. YOU MIGHT'VE SHIFTED ALL THE NERVES OUTTA YOUR HEAD AND NECK, BUT YOU'RE TOO MUCH OF A HORNDOG TO REMOVE 'EM FROM YOUR COCK, TOO.
HELL, THIS'LL PROBABLY TURN YOU ON.
SO MAYBE "MORTAL WEAPONS" CAN'T KILL YOU, BUT THEY CAN CAUSE A HELLUVA LOTTA PAIN.
NOW IF YOU LEAVE ME ALONE I'LL LET YOU KEEP WHATEVER DIGNITY YOU HAVE LEFT. DEAL?
DEAL.
FANTASTIC. THIS IS NEVER GONNA COME OUT. I LOVE THIS COAT.

DING
DING
UNBELIEVABLE. I JUST SWIPED THIS JACKET AND NOW IT'S COVERED IN DEMON SPLOOGE.
OLD ASS STAIN STICK'S JUST RUBBING THE GUNK IN MORE! GODDAMNIT!
YOU HAVE TO PAY FOR THAT. WE'RE NOT A CHARITY.
ROUGH DAY?
DON'T START WITH ME. I WILL LITERALLY POP YOUR HEAD LIKE A ZIT.
I'LL TAKE ONE OF THESE TOO.
DON'T SELL MANY OF THOSE.
CAN'T IMAGINE WHY.
THANK YOU FOR SHOPPING AT FAST MART.
GO DIE... AGAIN.

SINCE THERE ARE NO GOOD JOBS LEFT WE HAVE TO TAKE WHAT WE CAN GET. LIKE SERVING ROTTEN FOOD TO THE MISERABLY POOR.
YOU EVER WANNA GET TOGETHER MY VAN'S GOT A BED IN THE BACK. I RIPPED OUT ALL THE SEATS. FEEL ME?
THIS IS A JOKE, RIGHT?
MY PIZZA SUCKS!
SCREW YOU!
I GOT CALLED IN TO DEAL WITH ONE TRAGIC LOSER? NO OFFENSE.
SINCE YOU'RE HERE I'M GONNA TAKE OFF. WEAR THIS HAT OR YOU'RE FIRED. RITA'S IN CHARGE. IF YOU NEED ME JUST GIVE A LITTLE JINGLE JANGLE.
THAT TRAGIC LOSER IS A CUSTOMER. DON'T FORGET IT OR I'LL PICK SOME OTHER DEGENERATE OFF THE CURB TO DO YOUR JOB. AND WOULD IT KILL YOU TO WEAR A UNIFORM FOR ONCE?
YES. IT WOULD LITERALLY KILL ME.
HE'S GOT GENITAL WARTS, YOU KNOW.
SO DO I.
AWESOME.
PIZZA

SO, WHAT'S ON THE BACON PIZZA?
RANCID BACON MIXED WITH MY SPIT.
DING DING
SHIT. SHIT. SHIT! OF ALL THE PLACES WHY'D SHE HAVE TO COME HERE?
FRIEND OF YOURS?
I JUST SAW HER BROTHER GET KILLED FOR THE SECOND TIME.
BUMMER.
CAN WE GET SOME SERVICE OVER HERE?
YOU GO.
NU UH. I'M IN CHARGE. YOU GO.
I HOPE YOUR VAGINA FALLS OFF.

WHO ASKED YOU TO SIT DOWN?
I BROUGHT A PEACE OFFERING, CONNIE. FOR STICKING YOU WITH BARRY. HE'S JUST SUCH AN IDIOT.
OR I GUESS HE WAS.
YOUR BROTHER'S DEAD.
AND THAT'S HOW YOU TELL ME? BY OFFERING SOME MOLDY BREAD AND ROTTEN MEAT?
)COUGH(
HEY! IT'S THE BEST YOU'LL GET IN THIS TOWN.
THEN YOU EAT IT.
NO WAY. I'M NOT CRAZY. I'D RATHER STARVE.
)COUGH(
HE ALRIGHT?
HE'S FINE. AREN'T YOU, BABY?
)COUGH(
)COUGH(

I COULD GO IN THE BACK AND RUSTLE UP A CAN OF SOUP OR SOMETHING.
NO THANKS. I'VE LOST MY APPETITE.
WE'RE GOOD. LEAVE US ALONE.
WHATEVER.
ENJOY THE PIZZA.
NO.
BAM!
DENNIS. COME ON BABY. GET UP. GET UP.
OUT OF THE WAY.
WHAT ARE YOU DOING?

HATE ME ALL YOU WANT BUT HE NEEDS A DOCTOR AND YOU NEED MY HELP.
ALRIGHT. JUST BE CAREFUL. HE'S ALL I'VE GOT LEFT.
THERE'S A CLINIC NOT FAR FROM HERE. YOU STILL HAVE THAT CLUNKER OF YOURS?
PARKED RIGHT OUTSIDE.
GOOD, CUZ I DON'T WANNA DRAG HIM ACROSS THE BLACK ZONE.

OH GOD. HE ALMOST PUKED ON ME.
QUIT WHINING. SO YOU DIE A LITTLE.
GLURB!
CLICK
WHAT THE –
DON'T NEED YA ANYMORE. LATER SUCKA!
COME ON, WORK!
RMMRMMRMM
HAHAHAHAHAA
THIS ISN'T FUNNY!
YEAH. IT'S HILARIOUS.
JUST GIVE ME A PUSH.
I THINK I FOUND YOUR PROBLEM.

AND YOUR BOYFRIEND JUST HEAVED ON THE FLOOR AGAIN.
DAMN IT!
COME ON. IT'S A LITTLE FUNNY.
GLURG!
IT'S INFURIATING! WHAT DO WE DO NOW?
THERE'S NOT ANOTHER CAR IN SIGHT. NEAREST GAS STATION'S OVER THREE MILES AWAY. HE'LL BE DEAD BY THE TIME I GET BACK. SO, IT LOOKS LIKE WE'RE GONNA HAVE TO CARRY HIM ACROSS THE BLACK ZONE AFTER ALL.
ARE YOU KIDDING ME? YOU'VE GOTTA KNOW WHAT'S WAITING OUT THERE.
OF COURSE I DO.
NOT EVERY HELL BORN CREATURE ADAPTED TO LIVING IN THE SUBURBS. WILD HELLHOUNDS...
...AND UNCIVILIZED DEMONS ROAM THE DARKNESS OF THE BLACK ZONE.
THEY FEED ON THE FLESH OF TRESPASSERS.

WE DON'T HAVE ANY OTHER CHOICE. HELP ME WITH HIM.
THAT'S WHY WE HAVE TO STAY IN THE LIGHT WHERE IT'S SAFE.
I DUNNO. THE BLACK ZONE SOUNDS LIKE FUN TO ME.
YOU'RE CRAZY.
THINK WE'LL MAKE IT?
SURE.
ALL WE HAVE TO DO IS GET PAST FIVE FOOTBALL FIELDS WORTH OF SNARLING, DISGUSTING DEMONS AND HELLSPAWN.
WE'RE GONNA BE MAULED TO DEATH, AREN'T WE?
I MEAN...
THAT'S THE WORST CASE SCENARIO. WE MIGHT JUST GET HORRIBLY DISFIGURED.
BESIDES, WE'RE LIVING DURING THE APOCALYPSE. IT'S LITERALLY HELL ON EARTH.

GRRR
GROWL
HOW MUCH WORSE COULD DEATH BE?
AHWHOO

HURK!
NO. THEY'LL DEFINITELY HEAR HIS VOMITING THOUGH.
SEE CONNIE. THE BLACK ZONE'S A WALK IN THE PARK.
TOLD YOU. GET READY TO RUN.
GRRR
WE'VE BARELY GONE A HUNDRED FEET. NOW SHUT IT KATRINA, OR ARE YOU TRYING TO TIP OFF THE DEMON DOGS?
GROWL
GRAB DENNIS!
GRRR
HEAD BACK TO THE PIZZA SHOP.

THUNK!
WELL THAT DIDN'T WORK. GOOD THING THEY CAN'T STAND THE LIGHT OR WE'D BE GUTTED RIGHT NOW.
YELP
YELP
WHERE ARE YOU GOING?
JUST KEEP DENNIS ALIVE. I HAVE A PLAN.
A FEW MINUTES LATER.
EASY PIZZA
WHAT TOOK YOU SO LONG? DENNIS IS FADING FAST.
GIMME A BREAK. I HAD TO WRESTLE THESE AWAY FROM FAT RITA.
YEAH. ROTTEN FOOD. YOU LIKE THAT, HUH?
GROWL
GRRR

FETCH!
COME ON. THAT WON'T SIDETRACK THE DOGS FOR LONG.
AFTER SPRINTING A HUNDRED YARDS OR SO.
WHY ARE WE STOPPING?
DENNIS NEEDS A BREAK OR HIS HEART'LL EXPLODE.
YOU WITH ME BUDDY?
UGH.
WAKE UP! I'M NOT RISKING MY LIFE FOR YOU TO DIE!
I'M UP!
SMACK!

DENNIS IS GONNA FALL INTO A COMA ANY SECOND. WE NEED TO QUIT RESTING AND FIND A DOCTOR ASAP.
YOU'RE RIGHT. STAND HIM UP AND START WALKING.
GODDAMN IT. I THOUGHT WE HAD MORE TIME.
GRRR
KATRINA! HELP!
SNAP!

AAHHHHHH!!
CRACK!
GET TO THE CLINIC. I'LL KEEP THE DOGS BUSY.
BUT—
GO! IF I'M GONNA DIE IT BETTER MEAN SOMETHING.
THANK YOU. NOW WE'RE EVEN.
BULLSHIT. WE'RE WAY MORE THAN EVEN.
CAN'T OUTRUN THEM.

HOPE I CAN OUTJUMP THEM.
AAAIIIIIII!
GET OFF ME!
NICE DOGGIES. NO NEED TO RIP ME APART.

SQUISH!
YELP
SLAM

GOTTA TIME THIS RIGHT.
CRASH
SLAM
RRRR
ONLY ONE CHANCE TO SURVIVE. CAN'T SCREW IT UP.

DON'T DIE. DON'T DIE. DON'T DIE. DON'T DIE.
I MADE IT?
HOW THE HELL DID I MANAGE THAT?
MAYBE MY LUCK'S CHANGING.
DON'T BE AN IDIOT, KATRINA. THAT'S CRAZY TALK.

THE CLINIC.

KATRINA!

YOU HURT?
I'M FINE. HOW'S OUR BOY?
HE'S BEEN BETTER.

JEEZ DENNIS.

YOU LOOK TERRIBLE.
ALWAYS THE CHARMER.
GET COMFORTABLE.
THE NURSE MOVES LIKE MOLASSES. WE'RE NOT SEEING THE DOCTOR FOR A WHILE.

LATER. AFTER AN ETERNITY WAITING.
HOW LONG HAVE WE BEEN HERE?
FOREVER.
YUCK.
DENNIS IS GONNA DIE BEFORE WE EVEN GET INTO AN EXAM ROOM.
NO HE'S NOT.

WHAT'S TAKING SO LONG? MY FRIEND'S ABOUT TO KEEL OVER.
4700 PEOPLE LIVE WITHIN WALKING DISTANCE OF THIS CLINIC. ALMOST ALL OF THEM ARE GRAVELY ILL OR INJURED.
WHICH MEANS WE CAN'T JUST KISS THEIR BOO BOO AND SEND THEM ON THEIR MERRY WAY.
I GUARANTEE YOU MY FRIEND'S THE SICKEST PERSON IN THIS SHITHOLE. HE NEEDS A DOCTOR RIGHT NOW.
Betsy
GET YOUR HANDS OFF MY DESK.
MAKE ME.
SIT DOWN OR I'LL BLOW YOUR TITS OFF.
PULL THE TRIGGER. I DARE YOU.

BLAM
YOU BROKE MY NOSE!
THEN IT'S A GOOD THING YOU WORK IN A CLINIC.
I'LL BREAK LOTS MORE THAN THAT IF YOU DON'T BRING US INSIDE RIGHT NOW.
YOU WOULDN'T. I'M A HEALER.
TRY ME. I HAVE NO CONSCIENCE.
LET'S GO CONNIE. A ROOM OPENED UP.
FOLLOW ME. CUNT.
WATCH YOURSELF NOW. I WON'T THINK TWICE ABOUT CRACKING YOUR SKULL OPEN AND LEAVING YOU FOR THE HELLHOUNDS.

GROSS.
WHAT DID YOU EXPECT, CLUB MED?
SHE'S RIGHT. EVERYBODY IN. YOU TOO NURSE.
SIT.
DON'T MAKE ANY SUDDEN MOVEMENTS.
BLAM
BLAM
WHAT WAS THAT?!
NO IDEA.
STOMP
STOMP
STOMP
CREAK

GOOD EVENING. I'M DOCTOR—
WHAT IN THE NAME OF —
SORRY DOC, BUT WE'VE GOT AN EMERGENCY. OUR FRIEND WASN'T GONNA LAST ANOTHER FIVE MINUTES OUT THERE.
AND IF I HELP YOU, WHAT'S TO STOP EVERY DESPERATE PERSON FROM TRYING THE SAME TACTIC?
I SIMPLY CANNOT CATER TO INTIMIDATION.
UNDERSTANDABLE.
CHK! CHUK!
I'M THE ONLY DOCTOR WITHIN A TWENTY MILE RADIUS. KILL ME AND ONLY THE PATIENT WILL SUFFER.
GOT A POINT, DOC.

BANG!
WHUMP!

EXAMINE HIM OR I'LL KEEP SHOOTING PIECES OFF YOUR NURSE JOINT BY JOINT.
SHE BLEW OFF MY KNEECAP!
WE KNOW, BITCH. WE ALL SAW IT.
NOW WHAT'LL IT BE, DOC?
YOU HAVEN'T GIVEN ME MUCH OF A CHOICE.

THERE'S ALWAYS A CHOICE. JUST MIGHT NOT BE A GOOD ONE.

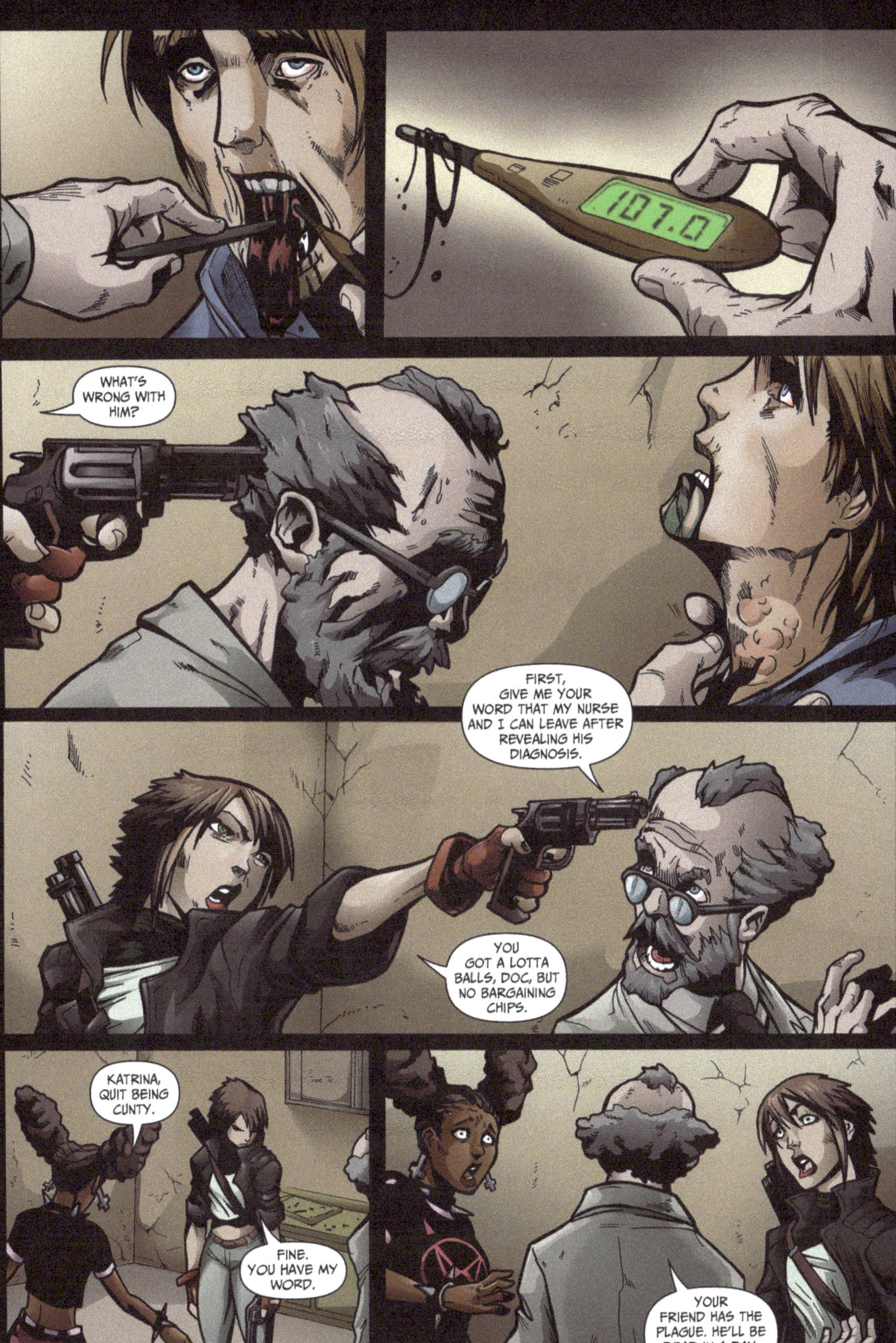

107.0
WHAT'S WRONG WITH HIM?
FIRST, GIVE ME YOUR WORD THAT MY NURSE AND I CAN LEAVE AFTER REVEALING HIS DIAGNOSIS.
YOU GOT A LOTTA BALLS, DOC, BUT NO BARGAINING CHIPS.
KATRINA, QUIT BEING CUNTY.
FINE. YOU HAVE MY WORD.
YOUR FRIEND HAS THE PLAGUE. HE'LL BE DEAD IN A DAY, TWO AT MOST.

THAT'S NOT TRUE. YOU'RE SCREWING WITH ME BECAUSE OF WHAT SHE DID TO YOUR NURSE. I DON'T EVEN LIKE HER. TELL ME IT'S SOMETHING ELSE. ANYTHING ELSE.
I'M QUITE CERTAIN HE SUFFERS FROM THE PLAGUE. MY RECOMMENDATION IS TO END HIS LIFE QUICKLY. OTHERWISE, HE'LL ENDURE AN EXCRUCIATINGLY PAINFUL DEATH.
YOU'RE LYING.
YOU'RE LYING!
CRACK!
CONNIE. STOP. HE'S NOT THE ENEMY.
HE'S LYING. HE'S LYING! HE HAS TO BE!
I'M NOT GONNA LET YOU DIE. HE'S WRONG. WE'LL GET A SECOND OPINION.
COUGH! COUGH!
YOU KNOW HE'S RIGHT. AND IF THAT'S WHAT I HAVE TO LOOK FORWARD TO, SHOOT ME IN THE HEAD RIGHT NOW. PLEASE.
I'M BEGGING YOU.

LEAVE.
FOR WHAT IT'S WORTH I'M SORRY.
I SWEAR. IF YOU SAY ANOTHER WORD.
I CAN'T LET YOU GO.
YOU HAVE TO.
STAY AS LONG AS YOU NEED.
I KNOW IT'S HARD, BUT I'M NOT STRONG ENOUGH TO DEAL WITH THAT MUCH PAIN. I'M GONNA DIE EITHER WAY. I WANT IT TO BE ON MY TERMS. MAKE IT QUICK. PLEASE.
OKAY.
IF YOU DON'T HAVE THE STOMACH I CAN—
NO. IF THIS IS WHAT HE WANTS I CAN HANDLE IT.
THINK I'VE REPENTED ENOUGH, CONNIE?
YES BABY. WE ALL HAVE.
I LOVE YOU WITH ALL MY HEART.
I LOVE YOU MORE THAN ANYTHING.

BANG!
I'M SORRY TOO.
I KNOW.
COME ON, WE COULD BOTH USE A DRINK.

LATER. AFTER KILLING A BOTTLE OF TEQUILA.
THERE'S STILL A SWIG LEFT.
YOU NEED IT MORE THAN ME.
CAN'T ARGUE THERE.
IT'S NOT GODDAMN FAIR.
WE SHOULD MARCH INTO HELL AND TELL THE DEVIL OFF FOR EVERYTHING HE'S PUT US THROUGH.
THAT'S THE BEST IDEA I'VE HEARD IN A LONG TIME. LET'S DO IT.
SERIOUSLY? I WAS JOKING.
NOTHING ABOUT THE LAST TWO YEARS HAS BEEN FAIR.
I'M NOT.
I COULD DEAL WITH NOT BEING RAPTURED, AND EVEN HELL ON EARTH, BUT PULLING THAT TRIGGER ON DENNIS IS JUST TOO MUCH BULLSHIT FOR ONE LIFETIME.
ARE YOU WITH ME?
ABSOLUTELY. I CAN'T WAIT TO HAVE IT OUT WITH THAT UGLY SONUVABITCH.

SHOULD YOU BE DRIVING?
THERE'S NOTHING TO HIT FOR MILES EXCEPT DEAD SHIT.
GOOD POINT. HOPE WE RUN OVER A WHOLE SLEW OF THEM ALONG THE WAY.
ME TOO.

HOW MUCH FURTHER?
DUNNO. WHEN I SEE A HUGE HOLE WITH DEMONS POURING OUT OF IT WE'LL STOP.
AND WHY DO YOU KEEP STARING AT THAT MAP LIKE DIRECTIONS TO THE RIFT ARE MAGICALLY GONNA APPEAR? THROW IT AWAY.
FINE. WE'LL JUST DRIVE AROUND IN CIRCLES FOR ANOTHER THREE DAYS THEN.
WHAT'S THAT SOUND?
WHOOSH!
INCOMING!
KABOOM

HOLY SHIT!
NOTHING.
WHAT ARE YOU LOOKING AT?
THEN HOW ABOUT YOU HELP ME DODGE THESE GODDAMN FIREBALLS!

AH HELL.
JUMP!
AAHHHHHH!!
I HATE THAT YOU'RE THE LAST THING I'M EVER GONNA SEE.
DITTO.

MY DEAR, I'M AFRAID YOU'VE STUMBLED INTO A BIT OF A WAR ZONE.
JESUS CHRIST THOMAS. NEVER THOUGHT I'D BE HAPPY TO SEE YOU.

WHO THE HELL ARE YOU, DEMON?
SO RUDE. NOT SURPRISING THOUGH. YOU ARE FRIENDS WITH MY KATRINA AFTER ALL.
WOULDN'T SAY WE'RE FRIENDS NECESSARILY.
THIS IS THOMAS, MY EX-LOVER. SWORE I'D KILL HIM IF HE EVER SHOWED HIS FACE AGAIN.
THOUGHT YOU MIGHT HAVE A CHANGE OF HEART AFTER I SAVED YOUR LIFE.
DON'T COUNT ON IT. WHAT ARE YOU UP TO IN THE MIDDLE OF THE DESERT ANYWAY?
FIGHTING.
AGAINST WHO?
THE DEVIL OF COURSE.
OR AS I LIKE TO CALL HIM, DEAR OLD DAD.

WELCOME TO THE RESISTANCE.
THESE DEMONS HAVE BROKEN SATAN'S CONTROL OVER THEM. WE HOPE TO GAIN FAVOR WITH GOD BY ENDING THIS WRETCHED APOCALYPSE ONCE AND FOR ALL.
SO BY ENDING THE APOCALYPSE YOU'LL WHAT? BE ABLE TO REENTER HEAVEN?
WELL I'VE NEVER BEEN TO HEAVEN PERSONALLY. BUT YES, THAT'S EXACTLY WHAT WE EXPECT.
I'VE WATCHED DEMONS RIP PEOPLE IN HALF FOR FUN. SEEMS LIKE THIS WOULD BE PARADISE FOR YOU.
WE ARE NOT TRULY LIKE THAT. SATAN HAS MANIPULATED MY KIND TOWARD HIS WICKED INCLINATIONS FOR MILLENIA. THERE IS SO MUCH YOU DO NOT UNDERSTAND.

SIT AND BECOME ENLIGHTENED.
WHAT'S THAT HUGE BOOK?
THE NECRONOMICON. IT TELLS THE TRUE ACCOUNTS OF EVENTS STRAIGHT FROM SATAN'S MOUTH.
SOME OF WHAT YOU KNOW IS TRUE OF COURSE.
MY FATHER WAS EXILED FROM HEAVEN EVEN BEFORE THE DAWN OF MAN.
HE DID TEMPT EVE WITH THE FIRST BITE OF FORBIDDEN SIN.
HE WAS RESPONSIBLE FOR THE DECADENCE OF SODOM AND GOMORRAH, THOUGH HE ALWAYS BELIEVED THEIR PUNISHMENT WAS A BIT EXCESSIVE.
BUT THAT IS WHERE YOUR RELIGIOUS TEXTS AND THE TRUTH DIVERGE.

FOR YOU SEE IT WAS ACTUALLY MY FATHER WHO TALKED TO MOSES AS THE BURNING BUSH.
AND WHILE GOD CONVINCED NOAH TO BUILD THE ARK, IT WAS MY FATHER WHO DROWNED THE WORLD.
IF THAT'S TRUE WHY DIDN'T GOD JUST SET US STRAIGHT?
HE TRIED.
BY INCARNATING INTO HUMAN FLESH HE TRIED TO WARN HUMANITY THAT THEY HAD BEEN DECEIVED.
BUT THE DEVIL EASILY CORRUPTED THOSE IN POWER.
AND YOUR ONE TRUE LORD WAS SLAIN.
WAIT WAIT WAIT!

ARE YOU REALLY TRYING TO STUFF THIS BULLSHIT DOWN OUR THROATS?
MY LOVE, I'VE SPOKEN TO SATAN AD NAUSEAM AND HEARD FIRST HAND ACCOUNTS OF GOD'S GLORY. YOU KNOW NOTHING ABOUT THE INNER WORKINGS OF THE AFTERLIFE.
SO EITHER HAVE FAITH IN MY HONESTY, OR GO BACK TO THAT DIRT HOLE TOWN OF YOURS. NOW, SHALL I FINISH?
YES, BUT YOU'RE ON WARNING.
NOTED.
LIKE ME, SATAN IS ABLE TO MANIPULATE HIS FORM.
AFTER THE CRUCIFIXION, HE WENT TO JESUS'S APOSTLES AND ALTERED SOME OF THE BIBLE'S STORIES BEFORE ADDING ONE OF HIS OWN.
A STORY OF DEATH, DESTRUCTION AND THE END OF THE WORLD.
WHICH WOULD BE BROUGHT ABOUT ONCE GOD OPENED SEVEN SEALS AND LAID JUDGMENT ON HUMANITY.
BUT THAT WAS ALL A LIE SET IN MOTION BY SATAN FOR HIS EVENTUAL CONQUEST OF BOTH EARTH AND HEAVEN.

WHICH IS WHY I BEGAN THIS REBELLION. AFTER TWO YEARS, MY FATHER'S CONQUEST OF THE WORLD IS COMPLETE. IT'S ONLY A MATTER OF TIME BEFORE HE TURNS HIS EYES TOWARD HEAVEN.
THAT SOUNDS LIKE MUMBO JUMBO TO ME.
EVERY WORD IS THE TRUTH.
AND TODAY WE TAKE THE FIGHT TO HELL... WITH THIS!
A PIDDLY DAGGER? WEAK SAUCE MAN.
IT WAS FORGED BY THE PRINCE OF EVIL HIMSELF. WHEN I PLUNGE THIS DEEP INTO HIS HEART THE DEVIL WILL BE NO MORE, THE APOCALYPSE WILL BE OVER, AND GOD WILL ALLOW US INTO HIS KINGDOM.
HUZZAH!
WHAT THE—
UH, BE RIGHT BACK KATRINA.
YOU!

THINK ABOUT IT. EVIL ONLY EXISTS BECAUSE MY FATHER FORCED IT UPON HUMANITY AT THE GARDEN OF EDEN.
THAT'S A NICE STORY AND ALL, BUT HOW DO YOU KNOW THAT ONCE THE DEVIL'S GONE THESE EVIL ASSHOLES WON'T JUST STICK AROUND FOREVER, FIGHTING GOD UNTIL THERE'S NOTHING LEFT OF HEAVEN OR EARTH?
THESE DEMONS USED TO BE THE BEAUTIFUL VOICE OF GOD, THEN SATAN CORRUPTED THEM. NOW THEY'RE MONSTERS.
THEY WANT TO GO HOME. WE ALL WANT TO GO HOME. ONCE THE DEVIL IS DEAD HE WILL HAVE NO CONTROL OVER THE HELLSPAWN.
THEY WILL RETURN TO GOD'S LEFT HAND, THE EVIL WILL VANISH FROM MEN'S HEARTS, AND EARTH WILL BECOME A PARADISE.
THEN I WANT TO HELP.
ME TOO!
IF KILLING THE DEVIL'S GONNA GET THE DICKHEADS AND MONSTERS OFF MY PLANET I'LL PLUNGE IN THE DAGGER MYSELF.
I HOPED YOU WOULD SAY THAT.

LATER, ON THE BATTLEFIELD.

THEY OUTNUMBER US TEN TO ONE.

WHY SWORDS AND AXES? CAN'T WE JUST USE GUNS?

YEAH. I COULD MOW DOWN THOUSANDS OF DEMONS WITH A HELL GUN.

THESE WEAPONS ARE ENCHANTED. THEY ARE THE ONLY WAY TO SLAY A DEMON.

THEN CAN I GET ONE?

MEN, IT IS TIME TO BEGIN THE FINAL BATTLE FOR BOTH OUR SOULS AND THOSE OF HUMANITY.

DON'T BOTHER ME WITH SUCH TRIFLES. I MUST ADDRESS MY TROOPS.

I WILL CASTRATE YOU.

JUST DO IT AFTER WE GET INTO HELL.

SHOULD YOU FALL TODAY REMEMBER THAT YOUR GALLANTRY WILL BE REWARDED IN HEAVEN!

ATTACK!

THIS IS BULLSHIT THOMAS!
WHERE'S THE FUN IN THAT?
I SERIOUSLY NEED A SWORD!
THE FUN IS IN SURVIVING. I'M STARTING TO FEEL LIKE AN IDIOT FOR LETTING YOU TALK ME INTO COMING HERE.
HAVE FAITH. IT WILL ALL WORK OUT.
JESUS CHRIST. HAVE YOU GONE RELIGIOUS ON ME?
HE HAS NOTHING TO DO WITH IT.
FANTASTIC. WE'RE ABOUT TO DIE AND YOU'VE CLEARLY GONE BATSHIT CRAZY.

NO YOU DON'T!
IF ANYBODY'S KILLING THIS DEMON...
...IT'S GONNA BE ME!

WE'VE COME A LONG WAY SINCE YOU THREATENED TO KILL ME.

I STILL RESERVE THAT RIGHT.

THIS IS YOURS.

KEEP IT. ONLY ONE WITH THE BLOOD OF A MORTAL CAN KILL THE DEVIL.

THEN HOW CAN YOU--

MY MOTHER IS MARYLYN MONROE.

NOW HURRY, WE MUST GET TO THE RIFT.

THANKS... AGAIN.

YOU'D DO THE SAME FOR ME.

NO I WOULDN'T.

FAIR ENOUGH.

WELL THOMAS, LOOKS LIKE WE GOT DEMON WEAPONS AFTER ALL.
AND IT'S WAY EASIER THAN USING OUR FISTS. WHO WOULDA THOUGHT?
SMARTASSES. JUST KEEP PUSHING FORWARD. THE RIFT IS JUST AHEAD.
WE'RE HERE. NOW WHAT?
JUMP!

IT'S THE ONLY WAY. HELL DOESN'T HAVE AN ELEVATOR.
ARE YOU CRAZY?
THERE IS NO WAY WE'RE DOING THAT.
SO YOU'D BETTER COME UP WITH A NEW PLAN!
KATRINA! NO!

THOMAS!
AHH!

GIVE ME YOUR HAND!
THAT SUCKED.
DID WE MAKE IT? ARE WE IN HELL?
SURE SMELLS LIKE HELL. NOW WE JUST GOTTA FIND THE DEVIL AND PLUNGE THIS DAGGER INTO HIS HEART WITHOUT THOMAS'S HELP. PIECE OF CAKE.
NO IDEA.
YEAH RIGHT. EXPLAIN TO ME HOW THE HELL WE'RE GONNA DO THAT?
MAYBE I CAN HELP.

BARRY?

WHAT HAVE YOU BEEN DOING DOWN HERE, BARRY?
I MAINLY TORTURE PEOPLE. HELL'S REALLY NOT THAT BAD IF YOU AREN'T A DAMNED SOUL.
BUT YOU'RE A ZOMBIE. HOW MUCH MORE DAMNED CAN SOMEBODY GET?
TECHNICALLY SPEAKING I'M A MONSTER. DOWN HERE THAT GIVES ME FREE REIGN TO DO JUST ABOUT ANYTHING.
I COULD SLIT KATRINA'S THROAT WITHOUT A SECOND THOUGHT. WOULDN'T THAT BE IRONIC?
NO, IT WOULDN'T.
WHICH WAY IS IT TO SATAN'S PALACE AGAIN?
ARE YOU SERIOUS?
FINE. I'LL TELL HER. JUST SHUT UP.
WHAT ARE YOU BABBLING ABOUT CONNIE?
WE SHOULD GO TO THE RIGHT.

AND HOW DO YOU KNOW THAT EXACTLY?
NO REASON. JUST DO IS ALL.
YOU'VE BEEN ACTING REALLY STRANGE LATELY, TELLING ME TO TRUST IN GOD AND MUMBLING TO YOURSELF.
YOU'RE A SATANIST FOR CHRIST SAKES.
TELL ME WHAT'S GOING ON RIGHT NOW!
I CAN'T! NOT YET AT LEAST.
THEN I'LL THROW YOU INTO THE RIVER!
I SHOULD PROBABLY ASK YOU TO STOP. SHE IS MY SISTER AFTER ALL.
SHUT IT BARRY!
SHE KNOWS BECAUSE OF ME, KATRINA.

DENNIS? THIS IS TOO GODDAMN MUCH.
CAN YOU LET GO OF ME NOW?

I CAME TO CONNIE OUTSIDE OF THOMAS'S TENT.
BABY, IT'S YOU!
AND YOU'RE AN ANGEL.
YES, BUT I STILL HAVE TO BREATHE.
I'M HERE TO HELP YOU END THE APOCALYPSE.
WAIT. IF YOU'RE AN ANGEL WHERE ARE YOUR WINGS?
DON'T HAVE THEM YET. I'VE GOTTA PERFORM A GREAT DEED FIRST.

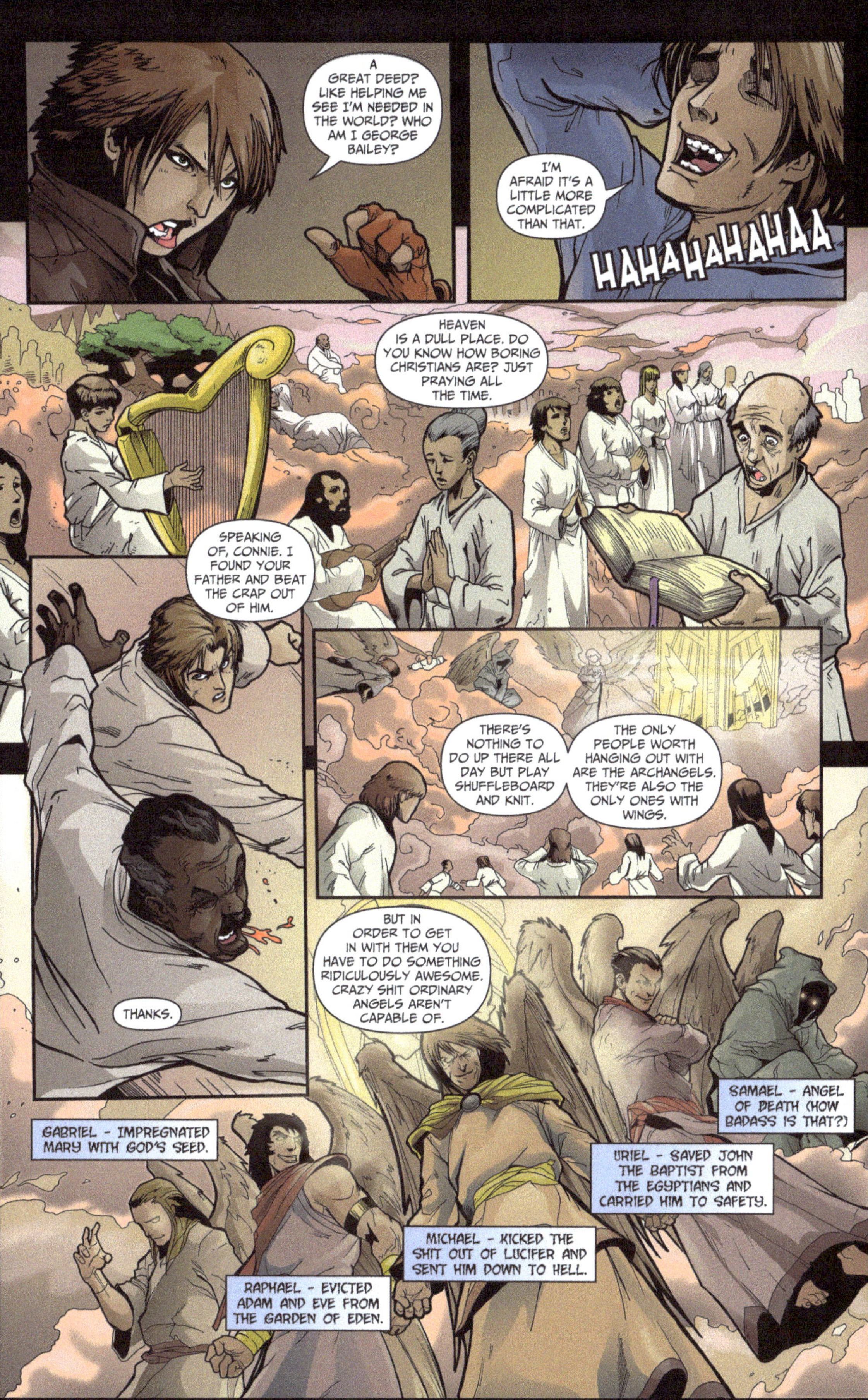

A GREAT DEED? LIKE HELPING ME SEE I'M NEEDED IN THE WORLD? WHO AM I GEORGE BAILEY?
I'M AFRAID IT'S A LITTLE MORE COMPLICATED THAN THAT.
HAHAHAHAHAA
HEAVEN IS A DULL PLACE. DO YOU KNOW HOW BORING CHRISTIANS ARE? JUST PRAYING ALL THE TIME.
SPEAKING OF, CONNIE. I FOUND YOUR FATHER AND BEAT THE CRAP OUT OF HIM.
THANKS.
THERE'S NOTHING TO DO UP THERE ALL DAY BUT PLAY SHUFFLEBOARD AND KNIT.
THE ONLY PEOPLE WORTH HANGING OUT WITH ARE THE ARCHANGELS. THEY'RE ALSO THE ONLY ONES WITH WINGS.
BUT IN ORDER TO GET IN WITH THEM YOU HAVE TO DO SOMETHING RIDICULOUSLY AWESOME. CRAZY SHIT ORDINARY ANGELS AREN'T CAPABLE OF.
SAMAEL - ANGEL OF DEATH (HOW BADASS IS THAT?)
GABRIEL - IMPREGNATED MARY WITH GOD'S SEED.
URIEL - SAVED JOHN THE BAPTIST FROM THE EGYPTIANS AND CARRIED HIM TO SAFETY.
MICHAEL - KICKED THE SHIT OUT OF LUCIFER AND SENT HIM DOWN TO HELL.
RAPHAEL - EVICTED ADAM AND EVE FROM THE GARDEN OF EDEN.

I SAW YOU PLANNED ON ENDING THE APOCALYPSE. I FIGURED THAT WOULD DEFINITELY BE A HUGE ENOUGH DEED TO BECOME AN ARCHANGEL.
SO I SNUCK DOWN HERE. THEY SAY GOD'S OMNIPOTENT BUT HE'S GOT PLENTY OF BLIND SPOTS IF YOU'RE CLEVER ENOUGH.
I PROTECTED YOU FROM THE FIREBALLS AS BEST I COULD.
BUT I COULDN'T CATCH THEM ALL.
I WAS SO JEALOUS WHEN THAT DEMON JERK GOT TO ACT LIKE A BIG HERO.
AW BABY. THAT'S SO SWEET.
YEAH, YEAH. VERY SWEET. GET ON WITH THE STORY.
I FOLLOWED YOU UNTIL THOMAS REVEALED HIS PLAN. I KNEW YOU'D NEVER SUCCEED WITHOUT ME.
AND IF YOU KILLED THE DEVIL I'D BE ABLE TO THROW IT IN THAT ASSHOLE MICHAEL'S SMUG FACE.
SO I APPEARED TO CONNIE AND HAVE BEEN WATCHING OUT FOR YOU EVER SINCE.

BORING. IF HEAVEN'S HALF AS DULL AS THAT STORY I FEEL REALLY SORRY FOR YOU BROTHER.
DOES THIS MEAN YOU'RE GONNA LEAD US TO THE DEVIL?
YES. I STUDIED THE PATH BEFORE LEAVING HEAVEN. BUT I WARN YOU IT'S NOT AN EASY ROAD AHEAD.
FANTASTIC, CUZ IF I DON'T KILL SOMETHING SOON I'M GONNA DIE OF BOREDOM.
THIS WAY?
AWESOME.
THAT'S RIGHT.
SHE'S STILL LIKE THAT, HUH?
YUP.
INFURIATING.
TELL ME ABOUT IT.

IT GUARDS THE WAY INTO SATAN'S PASS. BE CAREFUL. DEMONS ARE MORE POWERFUL IN HELL THAN ON EARTH.
PIECE OF CAKE.
TOLD YOU. EASY, PEEZY, LEMON SQUEEZY. WHAT'S NEXT?

THOSE DEMON DOGS ON THE SURFACE--THIS IS THEIR MOTHER. SHE'S AN ORNERY LITTLE BITCH WITH A VORACIOUS APPETITE. NOTHING GETS THROUGH THAT GATE AND ON TO SATAN'S PALACE WITHOUT HER APPROVAL.
NOT A PROBLEM. I'M SURE SHE'S DUMB JUST LIKE HER CHILDREN. COME HERE BARRY.
WHY?
I NEED A HAND.
OW!
SHHH! YOU'LL SPOOK HER.
SNIFF SNIFF
STAY BEHIND ME.
HERE GIRL. GOT A SMELLY MEAL FOR YOU.

FETCH!

CRACK

WHAT'S NEXT?

TWENTY LEGIONS OF ANGELIC GUARDS COULDN'T GET PAST HER.

HOW MANY MORE CHALLENGES TO GO?

I'VE SAID IT BEFORE AND I'LL SAY IT AGAIN, I'M BETTER THAN TWENTY LEGIONS OF ANGELS.

JUST ONE MORE, BUT IT'S PRETTY MUCH IMPOSSIBLE.

BRING IT ON.

ONLY CHARON'S ALLOWED TO CARRY THE GONDOLIER'S OAR. BOTH IT AND THE BOAT ARE ENCHANTED TO PREVENT THEM FROM BURNING IN THE LAKE.
CAN'T YOU JUST SWIM ACROSS?
THE LAKE PROBABLY WOULDN'T HURT BARRY OR ME, BUT OUR BODIES WOULD DISINTEGRATE BEFORE WE GOT TO THE OTHER SIDE. I GUESS WE COULD DO IT IN BURSTS, BUT THERE'S NO PLACE TO STOP AND BREAK ONCE WE LEAVE THE SHORE.
NOT THAT EASY. HE'LL ONLY BRING ACROSS SOULS PERSONALLY INVITED BY THE DEVIL HIMSELF.
YOU'RE NOT GIVING ME MUCH OF A CHOICE. I'LL JUST PAY THE SUMBITCH. WHAT'S IT COST, LIKE FIVE BUCKS?
WHO DARES REQUEST PASSAGE TO THE DARK LORD?
ME. AND I GUESS THESE ASSHOLES TOO.
NO BODY MAY PASS.
THAT'S JUST NOT FAIR. I DON'T LIKE YOUR ATTITUDE.

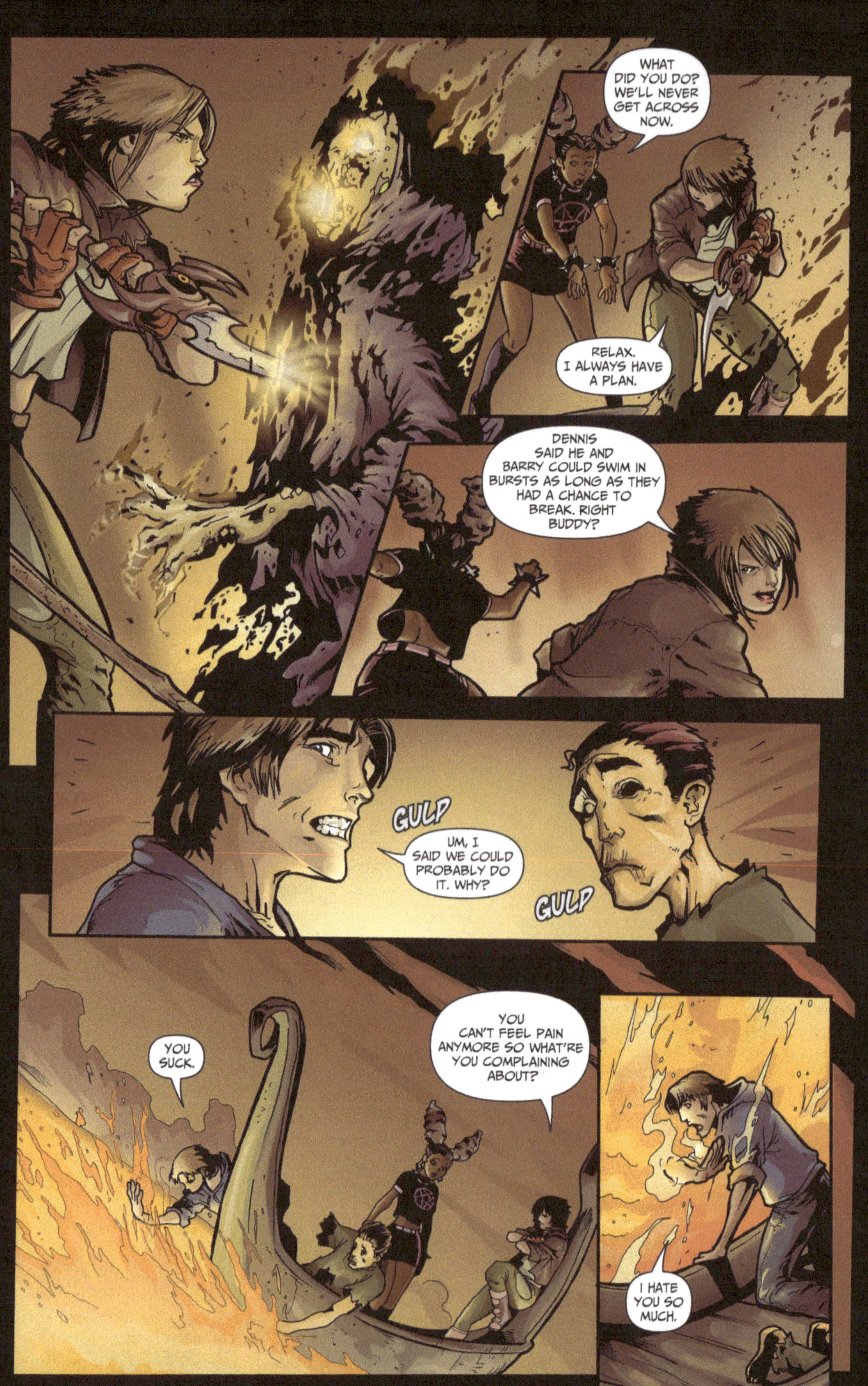

WHAT DID YOU DO? WE'LL NEVER GET ACROSS NOW.
RELAX. I ALWAYS HAVE A PLAN.
DENNIS SAID HE AND BARRY COULD SWIM IN BURSTS AS LONG AS THEY HAD A CHANCE TO BREAK. RIGHT BUDDY?
GULP
GULP
UM, I SAID WE COULD PROBABLY DO IT. WHY?
YOU SUCK.
YOU CAN'T FEEL PAIN ANYMORE SO WHAT'RE YOU COMPLAINING ABOUT?
I HATE YOU SO MUCH.

IF I EVER FIND MY ARM I'M BEATING YOU TO DEATH WITH IT.
BITCH, BITCH, BITCH.
YOU'RE LUCKY I'M NOT AN ARCHANGEL YET OR I'D LOP OFF YOUR HEAD SO FAST.
ALRIGHT. UP THE STAIRS, KILL THE DEVIL, END THE APOCALYPSE, GO HOME AND HAVE A SUNDAE. COULDN'T BE EASIER, RIGHT?
SUCK IT UP, DENNIS. WE'RE ABOUT TO KILL THE DEVIL. THEN YOU'LL GET YOUR WINGS. HOW ABOUT A LITTLE GRATITUDE?
REALLY JUST KATRINA'S GONNA KILL HIM. APPARENTLY "HUMAN BLOOD MUST COURSE THROUGH YOUR VEINS" TO KILL THE DEVIL OR SOME JUNK. BUT SHE'LL PROBABLY GIVE YOU ALL THE CREDIT.
YEAH, SHE'S A REAL SWEETHEART LIKE THAT.
AND WHAT DO I GET OUT OF THIS?
I PROMISE NOT TO RIP ANYTHING ELSE OFF YOU TODAY.
THAT'S THE NICEST THING YOU'VE EVER SAID TO ME.
DON'T MENTION IT.

THERE HE IS!
NO SHIT BARRY.
TIME TO END THIS.
KRUNCH
WELL WELL WELL.
IF IT ISN'T THE DISTINCT SMELL OF HUMANITY.
AND AN ANGEL. HOW VERY INTERESTING. GOD SENT A PEON TO COMMUNICATE WITH ME.
YOU THINK I WOULD HAVE EARNED A LITTLE MORE RESPECT AFTER TWO HUNDRED MILLENIA OF SERVICE.

ENOUGH. WE'RE HERE TO STOP YOUR RAMPAGE ON THE WORLD.

ARE YOU BABBLING ABOUT THE APOCALYPSE? WHOMEVER TOLD YOU I WAS RESPONSIBLE IS SORELY MISTAKEN.

YOUR HEAD GAMES DON'T WORK ON US. IF WE KILL YOU THE APOCALYPSE ENDS AND THERE WILL BE HEAVEN ON EARTH.

MY DEAR, IF YOU KILL ME THERE WON'T EVEN BE HEAVEN IN HEAVEN. I'LL LET YOU IN ON A SECRET.
HAVE ANY OF YOU EVER HEARD THE TERM ABSENTEE LANDLORD?

I HAVEN'T. IF THAT MEANS ANYTHING.

IT DOESN'T.
GOD CAN'T BE BOTHERED WITH THE WHOLE LOT OF YOU. HE'D BE JUST AS HAPPY IF NO SOULS ENTERED HIS KINGDOM FOR THE REST OF ETERNITY.
SINCE THE DAWN OF TIME HE'S WATCHED AS I'VE SCREWED WITH YOUR HEADS, MANIPULATED YOUR MINDS, AND DESTROYED YOUR SOULS. HAS HE ONCE TRIED TO STOP ME?

YES. BUT YOU HAD JESUS KILLED.
IS THAT WHAT YOU REALLY BELIEVE? HUMANITY DESTROYED JESUS, NOT I. AND LIKE A PETULANT CHILD GOD DESERTED YOU FOR THE LAST TWO THOUSAND YEARS WHILE HE SULKED, LEAVING NOTHING BUT HIS GREATEST JOKE.
FREE WILL. HE GRANTED EVERY PERSON THE ABILITY TO IGNORE HIS TEACHINGS, YET ETERNALLY PUNISHED THOSE THAT CHOSE NOT TO FOLLOW HIM BLINDLY.
WELL THEN, I'M GONNA USE MY FREE WILL TO JAM THIS DAGGER THROUGH YOUR HEART.
I WON'T STOP YOU. GOD HAS FORSAKEN ME. ALL I WANTED WAS TO SEE THE ELYSIAN FIELDS ONE MORE TIME. MAYBE IN MY NEXT LIFE I'LL BE A SIMPLE APPLE FARMER.
I WOULDN'T COUNT ON IT!
JUST BE WARNED. IF YOU STRIKE ME DOWN SOMETHING MUCH WORSE WILL TAKE MY PLACE.
MAYBE HE'S RIGHT KATRINA. WE SHOULD THINK ABOUT THIS.
I CAN'T BELIEVE YOU'RE FALLING FOR HIS BULLSHIT CONNIE! HE'S THE PRINCE OF ALL LIES. I WANT MY LIFE BACK!

HE JUST DROPPED LIKE A SACK OF POTATOES, DIDN'T HE?
IT'S OVER THEN?
DIDN'T GIVE UP A FIGHT OR NOTHIN'.
APPRECIATE YOU FINISHING DADDY OFF FOR ME HOWEVER. I DO SO HATE DIRTYING MY HANDS.
LOOKS THAT WAY.
NOT QUITE.
THOUGHT YOU WERE DEAD.
OF COURSE YOU DID, MY DEAR. THAT'S WHAT I WANTED YOU TO BELIEVE. DID YOU REALLY THINK YOU'D BE HERE IF IT HADN'T BEEN MY BIDDING?
THERE'S NO WAY YOU'D...
...BE ABLE TO KNOW WE'D MAKE IT HERE.

YOU REALLY HAVE SIMPLE MINDS, DON'T YOU? I'VE BEEN PLANNING THIS MOMENT SINCE THE APOCALYPSE BEGAN.
I JUST NEEDED THE PERFECT MORTAL. ONE WITH THE DRIVE AND SKILL TO FOLLOW MY PLAN THROUGH WITH SINGLE-MINDED FOCUS.
SOMEBODY WHO WOULD TAKE CARE OF MY FATHER WHILE I SHIFTED HIS FOCUS TOWARD MY RESISTANCE.
I DON'T THINK SO.
AND YOU WERE PERFECTION, MY DEAR. FOR MONTHS EVERY MOVE YOU'VE MADE HAS BEEN AT MY BEHEST.
YOU WERE SO EASILY MANIPULATED. AND NOW, MY LOVE, I WILL GIVE YOU EVERYTHING.
I HATE ALL DEAD SHIT, BUT YOU'RE AT THE TOP OF MY LIST.
YOU AIN'T PRETTY NO MORE.
FOOL! WE COULD HAVE RULED HELL TOGETHER.
NO THANKS. THIS PLACE IS A SHITHOLE.

I DON'T GET IT. WHY KILL YOUR DAD AT ALL?
BECAUSE I DESIRED CONTROL OF HELL AND DEAR OLD DADDY WANTED ME TO BE CONTENT WITH MIDDLE MANAGEMENT. I'M A VISIONARY. I DON'T SULLY MY GENIUS WITH TRIVIAL DAY TO DAY TASKS.
I GUESS WE CAN KISS PARADISE ON EARTH GOODBYE THEN.
I'M AFRAID SO. NOW THAT I'VE I'VE TAKEN CONTROL OF HELL A WHOLE NEW ERA OF CARNAGE WILL COMMENCE.
THAT DOES NOT SOUND GOOD FOR YOU GUYS.
DOESN'T SOUND GOOD FOR ANYBODY.
THE POWER, THE ABSOLUTE POWER!
YES! YES! THE OLD WAY OF DOING THINGS IS NO MORE. PREPARE FOR A NEW REIGN OF TERROR THAT WILL TOPPLE HEAVEN ITSELF!

UH OH.
THERE GOES HUMANITY.

IS EVERYTHING TURNING WHITE?

I DON'T
LIKE THIS ONE
BIT.

DID I
JUST STROKE
OUT?

NO MY CHILD.

THIS IS HEAVEN.
I'M SO SCREWED.

YOU GOT THAT RIGHT DENNIS. WHAT RIGHT DID YOU HAVE LEADING THESE CHIPPIES INTO HELL?
WHAT THE SHIT'S A CHIPPY?
HOW STUPID CAN YOU IDIOTS BE?!
CALM YOURSELF MICHAEL. THEY KNEW NOT WHAT WOULD BE UNLEASHED UPON US.
SO YOU'RE GOD HUH?
YES MY CHILD.
AND THAT'S THE DEVIL SITTING NEXT TO YOU.
I AM MICHAEL. THE MOST POWERFUL OF ALL THE ARCHANGELS.
PLEASE, YOU KILLED ME. DROP THE FORMALITIES AND CALL ME LUCIFER.
APPRECIATE IT, LOU. YOU SEEM LESS NUTTY THAN LAST TIME I SAW YOU.
APOLOGIZES. TWO HUNDRED MILLENNIA IN HELL DOES CRAZY THINGS TO THE BRAIN.
SECOND. SECOND MOST POWERFUL. NEXT TO ME.
YOU? THE MOST POWERFUL ARCHANGEL? YOU'RE A FAT SACK OF SHIT WHO GOT MURDERED BY A MORTAL.
I BELIEVE IT. THAT PLACE IS AWFUL. WHO'S THE OTHER ASSHOLE?
BOYS, BOYS, BOYS, WHIP 'EM OUT AND COMPARE OR SHUT UP.
AND WHILE YOU'RE AT IT, HOW ABOUT TELLING ME WHAT WE'RE DOING HERE?

THERE IS A WAR RAGING, KATRINA. A WAR YOU BEGAN.
IT'S SUCH A COP OUT TO BLAME ME FOR THIS.
MOMENTS AFTER I DIED, THOMAS TOOK CONTROL OF HELL AND ATTACKED HEAVEN.
TRUTH BE TOLD, MOST ANGELS ARE HUGE PUSSIES. DO YOU HAVE ANY IDEA THE LITANY OF INFRACTIONS A PERSON CAN'T COMMIT IN ORDER TO PASS THROUGH THE NEEDLE'S EYE?
THE MEEK COULDN'T SWING A SWORD IF THEIR AFTERLIVES DEPENDED ON IT.
OUR ARMY WON'T LAST ANOTHER HOUR OF THIS ONSLAUGHT. WE NEED YOUR HELP.
NOT UNTIL THE BIG MAN ANSWERS A QUESTION FOR ME.
WHO ARE YOU TO DEMAND ANYTHING FROM GOD ALMIGHTY? WE DON'T HAVE TIME—
RELAX, MICHAEL. I CREATED KATRINA TO BE INQUISITIVE AND WILL ACQUIESCE TO HER DEMAND.
SUCK IT, ASSHOLE.
YOU WISH TO KNOW WHY THE APOCALYPSE BEGAN.
ACTUALLY I JUST WANNA KNOW WHO'S RESPONSIBLE. YOU? LUCIFER? THOMAS?
SERIOUSLY, IT'S ALL REALLY CONFUSING.
THE APOCALYPSE WAS AN INEVITABLE EVENTUALITY OF A FATAL FLAW IN THE HUMAN CONDITION. A FATAL FLAW THAT I AS THEIR CREATOR AM RESPONSIBLE FOR.

QUIT WITH THE FLOWERY BULLSHIT. WHO OPENED THE HELL RIFT AND UNLEASHED MONSTERS ON EARTH?
THAT IS A LONG AND COMPLICATED EXPLANATION. I ASK YOU TRUST IT WAS THE ONLY POSSIBLE SOLUTION TO AN IMPOSSIBLE PROBLEM.
TRUST YOU? I'VE BEEN FIGHTING OFF UNDEAD ASSHOLES FOR TWO YEARS. EVERYBODY I'VE EVER CARED ABOUT IS DEAD.
I DON'T TRUST EITHER OF YOU ONE IOTA. NOW TELL ME EVERYTHING OR I'M NOT LIFTING A FINGER TO HELP OUT.
VERY WELL. LONG AGO I MADE A DEAL WITH LUCIFER. IF HE HELD HELL TOGETHER FOR THREE HUNDRED MILLENIA I WOULD ALLOW HIM BACK INTO HEAVEN.
IT WASN'T SO MUCH A DEAL AS AN ULTIMATUM. NOT LIKE I HAD A LOT OF CHOICE IN THE MATTER.
YOU ALWAYS HAVE A CHOICE.
RIGHT. EITHER TAKE OVER HELL OR BE DELETED FROM EXISTENCE.
THAT DOESN'T SEEM LIKE MUCH OF A CHOICE TO ME.
ME EITHER, WHICH IS WHY I ACCEPTED.
FOR THE FIRST NINETY NINE HUNDRED YEARS OF HUMAN EXISTENCE IT WAS PRETTY EASY. LIFE EXPECTANCY WAS LOW AND INFANT MORTALITY WAS HIGH.
PEOPLE FEARED GOD AND GENERALLY COULDN'T COMMIT MANY SINS BEFORE THEY DIED.

BUT AFTER THE INVENTION OF CARS, PLANES, AND THE INTERNET HUMANITY COULD DO AND SEE THINGS THEIR ANCESTORS COULDN'T EVEN IMAGINE.
HAVE YOU EVER SEEN A DONKEY SHOW? THAT'S SIX MORTAL SINS IN UNDER AN HOUR. ONE'S ENOUGH TO BOOK A TRIP TO HELL.
SO I BEGAN THE APOCALYPSE TO EASE HIS BURDEN. HE WAS, AFTER ALL, MY OLDEST FRIEND. I DIDN'T WISH TO SEE HIM SUFFER.
LET ME GET THIS STRAIGHT. YOU UNLEASHED HELL ON EARTH, NOT THE DEVIL. AND YOU DID IT BECAUSE--
CORRECT, BECAUSE THERE WAS SIMPLY NO ROOM LEFT IN HELL. THE ADDED BONUS BEING HUMANITY MIGHT REALIZE THE ERROR OF THEIR WAYS AND ATONE FOR CENTURIES OF HEDONISTIC BEHAVIOR.
COMBINE THAT WITH THE FACT PENICILLIN ALLOWED PEOPLE TO LIVE FOREVER AND ALL THEIR SINS ADDED UP TO AN ETERNITY IN HELL. IT GOT INCREDIBLY CROWDED AND I COULDN'T KEEP ORDER ANY MORE.
PRETTY MESSED UP RIGHT?
THAT'S EXACTLY WHAT I WAS THINKING. MAN, NOW I'M A LITTLE SORRY I KILLED YOU.
WELL THANK YOU MY DEAR.
SO THERE'S NO WAY TO SUCK ALL THOSE CREEPY CRAWLERS BACK INTO HELL?
UNFORTUNATELY, THAT COURSE OF ACTION MUST BE MUTUALLY AGREED UPON BY BOTH GOD AND THE DEVIL. A TERRIBLE OVERSIGHT WHICH ESSENTIALLY LED TO OUR CURRENT PREDICAMENT.

LUCIFER WAS A LOYAL SUBJECT UNTIL THE VERY END. HE UNDERSTOOD THE DELICATE BALANCE BETWEEN HEAVEN AND HELL; THAT ONE COULD NOT EXIST WITHOUT THE OTHER.
YOU'RE KIND OF DUMB FOR AN OMNISCIENT BEING. WHY WOULD YOU DO THAT?
HE ASSUMED I WOULD BE THERE TO CARRY OUT HIS ORDERS UNTIL TIME STOPPED... OR HE COULD FIND ANOTHER SUCKER TO REPLACE ME.
YOU'RE A BETTER MAN THAT ME, LOU. I WOULD'VE GONE POSTAL AND KAMIKAZED HEAVEN EONS AGO.
PROBABLY WHY I WAS SUCH A POWERFUL ALLY.
THIS THOMAS, HOWEVER, IS A PLAGUE. HE WAS TROUBLE FROM THE START.
I BEGGED GOD TO LET ME LOP OFF HIS HEAD YEARS AGO. NOW IT'S TOO LATE.

SINCE THOMAS BECAME THE DEVIL HE'S GATHERED EVERY PITIFUL SOUL IN HELL TO MARCH AGAINST OUR RANKS.
SO-
HE HAS A SPECIAL AFFINITY FOR YOU I'LL NEVER UNDERSTAND. SINCE WE CAN'T APPROACH HIM YOU MUST GET CLOSE AND KILL THE DEVIL.
OKAY.
REALLY? THAT WAS EASY.
NO MATTER HOW BIG AN ASSHOLE GOD IS, THOMAS IS WORSE.
HE'S DESTROYING HEAVEN, SENT ZOMBIES TO KILL BARRY, TRICKED US INTO KILLING LUCIFER, AND MANIPULATED ME INTO SLEEPING WITH HIM. HE'S GOTTA DIE.
WHERE'S HE HIDING OUT?
THOMAS SITS ON A THRONE AT THE REAR OF THE BATTLE, WATCHING HEAVEN CRUMBLE.
AWESOME. THOMAS'S HEAD COMING RIGHT UP.
WAIT. YOU CAN'T KILL THE DEVIL WITHOUT AN ENCHANTED WEAPON.

THOMAS THREW IT INTO THE MOLTEN LAVA OF HELL. IN HINDSIGHT I SHOULD HAVE DONE THAT EONS AGO.
DUH. I'VE GOTTA FIND THAT STUPID DAGGER AGAIN.
FAN-FRIGGIN-TASTIC. HOW THEN?
WITH THIS SWORD FORGED BY GOD HIMSELF. ONLY THE WORTHY WILL BE ABLE TO WIELD IT.
HERE GOES NOTHING.
THIS SWORD IS AWESOME.

COME ON EVERYBODY. LET'S GO KILL THE DEVIL.
NOT A CHANCE. DENNIS CAN'T BE TRUSTED AND BARRY'LL JUST BUNGLE IT UP. YOU CAN HAVE CONNIE, I GUESS.
DON'T I GET A SWORD OR SOMETHING?
YOU CAN HAVE THIS. MAYBE IT'LL PROTECT YOU.
I'D RATHER HAVE A WEAPON.
TOUGH TITTIES.
I PROMISE THIS IS THE LAST TIME YOU'LL EVER HAVE TO HUG ME GOODBYE.
WHAT CAN WE DO?
YOU'VE DONE ENOUGH. IF EITHER OF YOU STEP FOOT ON THE BATTLEFIELD I'LL END YOUR LIVES MYSELF. COME LUCIFER.
I'M NOT REALLY IN FIGHTING SHAPE, BUT LET'S GIVE IT A GO.
THIS IS BULLSHIT.
BYE MIKEY!
FOLLOW ME BARRY. WE'RE GONNA HELP.
BUT YOU HEARD HIM. I DON'T WANNA DIE!
YOU'RE ALREADY DEAD DUMMY.
OH, RIGHT.

THIS SWORD CUTS THROUGH HELLSPAWN LIKE BUTTER. IT'S MESSING UP MY BACK THOUGH.
BITCH, BITCH, BITCH. I'M FIGHTING DEMONS WITH A STUPID ROSARY. I'LL TRADE YOU.
NO THANKS.
THAT'S WHAT I THOUGHT. BEHIND YOU.
THERE WE GO. THIS IS MORE LIKE IT.
BETTER?
MUCH.
GOOD. NOW QUIT YOUR WHINING.
AND GET READY TO SWING THAT HAMMER RIGHT ABOUT NOW.

HISSS
HISSS
SHUT UP, UGLY!
LET'S DO THIS.

THUD!
WHAT A FUN LITTLE WARM UP.
YOU'RE A MORON.

I'M SCARED.
YOU'VE ALREADY DIED TWICE. WHAT'S THE WORST THAT HAPPENS?
DYING A THIRD TIME OBVIOUSLY!
I TOLD YOU NOT TO INTERFERE DENNIS! GET OUT OF HERE.
WE'RE NOT GOING ANYWHERE.
SPEAK FOR YOURSELF.
GRAB THAT AX AND FOLLOW ME BARRY!
BUT I—
DO IT!
YOU'RE GOING TO GET ME KILLED!
NO, I'M GONNA SAVE YOUR LIFE!

SMASH ITS HEAD IN BARRY!
I DON'T WANNA.
GROSS!!!
NOW!
THAT WAS... EXHAUSTING.
OKAY. YOU'RE NOT USELESS DENNIS.
TOLD YOU.
DON'T GET COCKY. THERE'S STILL A LOT OF FIGHTING LEFT TO BE DONE.
I JUST PEED MYSELF.

SO YOU'RE JUST GONNA STROLL UP AND ASK NICELY IF YOU CAN SEE THE DEVIL?
IT'S AS GOOD AS ANY OTHER PLAN.
DOUBTFUL.
TURN BACK NOW MORTAL.
SAVE IT ASSTARD. I'M HERE TO SEE THOMAS.
THERE IS NO THOMAS HERE LITTLE GIRL.
THE DEVIL. ALRIGHT. WE'RE HERE TO SEE THE DEVIL. LET US THROUGH.
LEAVE BEFORE I RIP YOU APART.
YOU'RE PRETTY COCKY BUDDY. TELL YOU WHAT.
I'LL CUT YOU IN HALF AND FIND HIM MYSELF.
THAT'S NOT GONNA END WELL.

MAYBE THIS WASN'T MY BEST IDEA.
YOU THINK!
WAIT!
MY DEAR, I'M SO GLAD YOU'VE COME. WHEN YOU DISAPPEARED I FEARED THE WORSE.
I THOUGHT THE GOOD LORD MIGHT'VE PUNISHED YOU FOR KILLING HIS LOYAL DISCIPLE.
LET THEM PASS.
NOPE. GOD JUST WANTED TO HAVE A LITTLE CHAT. YOU KNOW, WOMAN TO OMNISCIENT BEING.
BUT HE BORED ME SO NOW I'M BACK TO SEE YOU.
EWW.

COME NOW KATRINA. DON'T MAKE THAT FACE. AREN'T YOU HAPPY TO SEE ME?

I DIDN'T THINK YOU WERE ALL THAT ATTRACTIVE AS A REGULAR LOOKING DEMON. NOW YOU'RE DOWNRIGHT HIDEOUS.

I DON'T HAVE TO ASSUME THIS FORM.

I CAN BECOME ANYONE OR ANYTHING YOU DESIRE.

JUST TELL ME WHAT YOU WANT.

THEN YOU'LL HAVE TO KILL ME.

THAT WE CAN DO. NOW CONNIE!

THE ONLY THING I WANT IS FOR YOU TO DROP DEAD.

FOOLS!

CONNIE.
CONNIE. COME ON.
GET UP.

I ALWAYS
KNEW YOU WERE
GONNA GET ME
KILLED.

I SHOULD HAVE KNOWN YOU WOULD BETRAY ME. I'VE BEEN SO BLIND.
YOU LOOK FRIGHTENED. AND YOU SHOULD BE. YOU'LL NEVER MAKE IT TO YOUR SWORD BEFORE I REACH YOU.
THAT SOUNDS LIKE A CHALLENGE.
OUT OF MY WAY!
DON'T TOUCH THE MORTAL. LEAVE HER FOR ME!

TSK, TSK TSK.
SO CLOSE.
UNFORTUNATELY CLOSE JUST ISN'T GOOD ENOUGH. NOW I WILL ABSORB YOU INTO MYSELF. WE WILL BE TOGETHER FOREVER AND YOU WILL NEVER BETRAY ME AGAIN.
SAY YOUR PRAYERS.
GREAT IDEA.
UUHHJJH.

WHAT HAVE YOU DONE TO ME?
NOTHING YET, BUT I'M ABOUT TO KILL YOU.
PLEASE KATRINA. SPARE ME.
AFTER ALL THIS YOU WANT ME TO BE MERCIFUL?
WHY THE HELL WOULD I DO THAT?
Because I love you.

CRAP.

THE MONSTERS OF HELL ARE NOW YOURS TO COMMAND.

I WANT THEM ALL BACK WHERE THEY BELONG.

THANK YOU MY CHILD. YOU'VE DONE WONDERFULLY.

SHE DID IT.
IN THAT MOMENT HUMANITY'S LONG NIGHTMARE WAS OVER. HEAVEN WAS ONCE AGAIN SAFE.
HELLSPAWN WERE SUCKED BACK INTO THE ABYSS.

THE RIFT IN THE DESERT CLOSED FOREVER.
FOR HIS SERVICE BARRY WAS ALLOWED TO LIVE OUT THE REST OF HIS LIFE IN HUMAN FORM.
IT LASTED TWO WEEKS BEFORE HE ELECTROCUTED HIMSELF IN THE TUB.
EVEN THOUGH SHE DIED, EVERYTHING WORKED OUT FOR CONNIE. SHE WAS REUNITED WITH DENNIS IN HEAVEN.
THEY'D NEVER BE AWAY FROM EACH OTHER AGAIN.
MICHAEL EVEN THOUGHT SO MUCH OF DENNIS THAT HE WAS PROMOTED TO ARCHANGEL.
THE WORLD RETURNED TO NORMAL. EVENTUALLY PEOPLE BEGAN TO FORGET ABOUT THE APOCALYPSE.
ONLY ONE PERSON DIDN'T MAKE OUT IN THIS WHOLE DEAL.

THAT WOULD BE ME, KATRINA.
THE NEW DEVIL.
I'M STUCK HERE WITH THE SHIT I HATE MOST FOR ALL ETERNITY.
THAT'S WHAT YOU GET FOR BEING A HERO KIDS.
NEVER AGAIN.
DON'T BE SO SURE. THREE HUNDRED MILLENNIA IS A VERY LONG TIME.

PINUP ARTISTS

1. CHRIS THOMASMA
2. BRADLEY SHERIDAN
3. NICOLAS TOURIS
4. ANGELA FULLARD
5. KATIE HENDERSON
6. GREG WORONCHAK
7. SEAN MCFARLAND
   AND AMANDA SOUSA MACHADO
8. ERIK LERVOLD
9. PATCH SILVER
10. PATCH SILVER
11. BILL WALKO
12. ALLISON BARROWS

THANK YOU TO ALL THE WONDERFUL ARTISTS WHO CREATED CONTENT FOR THIS BOOK.

AND THANK YOU, AMAZING READER, FOR SUPPORTING IT.

IT MEANS THE WORLD TO ME.

Weekly NEWS
Demons
Twitter: @GregWoronchak
gregworonchak.deviantart.com

KATRINA
HATES THE DEAD
WP

KATRINA
HATES THE DEAD

EASY
Pizza
WALKO

CONNIE
KATRINA:
JACKET OFF
J
THOMAS

RITA.
DENNIS
RONALD
JM.

DEMON DOG

ZOMBIES

MINOTAUR

GENERIC GHOST.

ISSUE #3

PAGE 7 - 5 PANELS

PANEL 1 - THOMAS SITS DOWN ON ONE OF THE PILLOWS
NEXT TO A DEMON WHO'S HOLDING A HUGE, ANCIENT BOOK.

THOMAS - SIT AND BECOME ENLIGHTENED.

KATRINA - WHAT'S THAT HUGE BOOK?

PANEL 2 - KATRINA AND CONNIE SIT ON PILLOWS AS THOMAS
GRABS THE BOOK FROM THE DEMON.

THOMAS - THE NECRONOMICON. IT TELLS THE TRUE
ACCOUNTS OF EVENTS STRAIGHT FROM SATAN'S MOUTH.

FLASHBACK

PANEL 3 - SATAN FALLS FROM HEAVEN. WE'RE WATCHING A
STREAK FALL IN THE SKY. WE SHOULD BE FAR AWAY HERE.
THERE SHOULD BE A STREAK BEHIND HIM.

THOMAS- SOME OF WHAT YOU KNOW IS TRUE OF COURSE.

THOMAS- MY FATHER WAS EXILED FROM HEAVEN EVEN BEFORE
THE DAWN OF MAN.

PANEL 4 - A SNAKE HISSES UP TO EVE. IT'S WRAPPED
HIMSELF AROUND AN APPLE. HIS FORKED TONGUE STICKS OUT.

THOMAS - HE DID TEMPT EVE WITH THE FIRST BITE OF
FORBIDDEN SIN.

PANEL 5 - FIREBALLS DESTROY SODOM AND GOMORRAH.
WE'RE ON A STREET CORNER WATCHING THE FIREBALLS
FALL FROM THE SKY IN THE BACKGROUND. PEOPLE RUN FROM
THE FIREBALLS. HOUSES FLAME. IT'S BEDLAM. THIS IS
THOUSANDS OF YEARS AGO SO THE HOUSES SHOULD BE OLD,
YET DESTROYED.

THOMAS- HE WAS RESPONSIBLE FOR THE DECADENCE OF
SODOM AND GOMORRAH, THOUGH HE ALWAYS BELIEVED
THEIR PUNISHMENT WAS A BIT EXCESSIVE.

THOMAS - BUT THAT IS WHERE YOUR RELIGIOUS TEXTS
AND THE TRUTH DIVERGE.

ISSUE #3, PAGE 7 SKETCH TO COLORS

SKETCH

PENCIL

INK

COLOR

ALSO FROM  PRESS

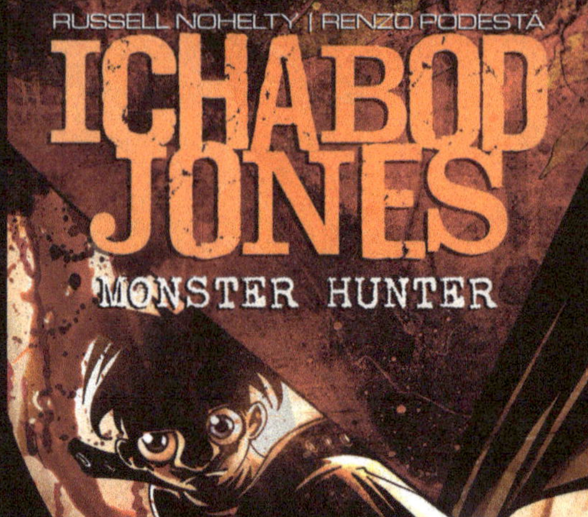
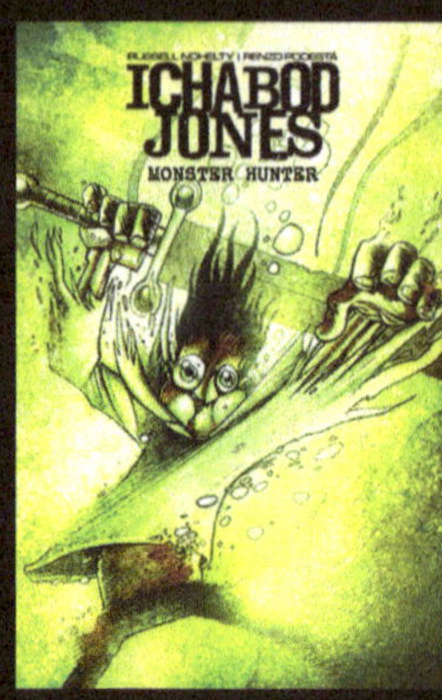
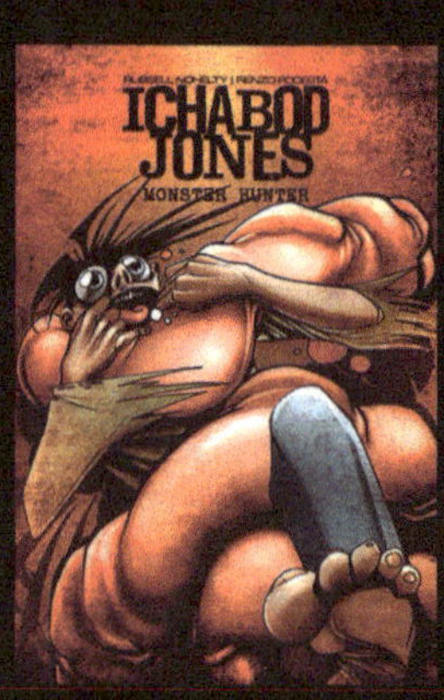

ICHABOD JONES: MONSTER HUNTER

ICHABOD JONES IS A DERANGED, MENTALLY UNSTABLE PSYCHOPATH. HE'S ALSO ON A MISSION TO SAVE THE WORLD— AT LEAST THAT'S WHAT THE BOSSY VOICE IN HIS HEAD TELLS HIM. THE SAME VOICE THAT TOLD HIM HIS CAUSE WAS RIGHTEOUS. THE SAME VOICE THAT TAUGHT HIM TO KILL. THE SAME VOICE THAT CONVINCED ICHABOD HIS VICTIMS WERE MONSTERS. THE SAME VOICE THAT A JURY USED TO FIND HIM INSANE.

NOW, HE'S WOKEN UP IN THE APOCALYPSE AND MUST USE ALL HIS BRUTAL TRAINING TO FULFILL HIS DESTINY – RIDDING THE WORLD OF MONSTERS BY SLAYING EVERY ONE HE COMES ACROSS.

OF COURSE HE'S STILL A PSYCHOPATH, SO WHO KNOWS IF IT'S ALL IN HIS HEAD.